NONE
STOOD
TALLER
The Final Year

Peter Turnham

From the D-Day landings to the VE-Day celebrations.
The final year of one woman's remarkable story.

Cover design and interior formatting by JD Smith Design

Copyright © 2021 Peter Turnham

All rights reserved

ISBN No: 978-1-9160979-7-1 (paperback)
978-1-9160979-8-8 (e-book)

Publisher: P&C Turnham
www.peterturnhamauthor.com

Front Cover
Front cover image is of Westminster Bridge, looking towards the Houses of
Parliament.
Photograph taken in 1945.
The iconic scene is depicted in detail in Chapter Thirty-Five.

Back cover
Back cover image is of VE-Day celebrations in Whitehall, looking towards the
Cenotaph.
Photograph taken 8th of May 1945
This scene is depicted in Chapter Forty-Eight.

Also by Peter Turnham

"None Stood Taller"
From the ashes of the Blitz to the D-Day landings.
One woman's remarkable story.

"Autumn Daffodils – Charlie's Story"
We are all the product of the past, but the future is ours.

"Autumn Daffodils – Joanna's Story"
Joanna will break your heart, but you will forgive her.

Acknowledgements

To my wife Carol,
my spell- and grammar-check,
my editor and IT consultant,
my indispensable other half.

Dedication

This book is dedicated to my late parents
and all those of the 'greatest generation'.
When the call came, they were not found wanting.

Table of contents

Introduction		1
The Story So Far		2
Chapter One	The Morning After	3
Chapter Two	The Exquisite Moment	23
Chapter Three	Things Left Unsaid	32
Chapter Four	Our Proudest Moment	42
Chapter Five	The Calm Before The Storm	59
Chapter Six	The Phone Call	68
Chapter Seven	St Hugh's Military Hospital	86
Chapter Eight	The Concert	95
Chapter Nine	Edward's Confusion	106
Chapter Ten	Dotty's Back	115
Chapter Eleven	The V1 Threat	124
Chapter Twelve	Lady Elizabeth	136
Chapter Thirteen	Fiona's Unbridled Joy	151
Chapter Fourteen	The V2 Threat	162
Chapter Fifteen	Gran's Bad Turn	173
Chapter Sixteen	Collective Genius	182
Chapter Seventeen	Dark Secrets	189
Chapter Eighteen	Elizabeth Goes To Hut 3	203
Chapter Nineteen	Middlebourne On The War Front	212

Chapter Twenty	Operation Goodwood	222
Chapter Twenty-One	Return From Arisaig	233
Chapter Twenty-Two	Girls' Night Out	243
Chapter Twenty-Three	The Other Woman	257
Chapter Twenty-Four	Wedding Plans	264
Chapter Twenty-Five	Fiona's Big Day	271
Chapter Twenty-Six	The Telegram	284
Chapter Twenty-Seven	The Funeral	294
Chapter Twenty-Eight	The Briefing	302
Chapter Twenty-Nine	A Letter From The Grave	312
Chapter Thirty	Market Garden	319
Chapter Thirty-One	Greg Norton's News	327
Chapter Thirty-Two	Operation Cormorant	334
Chapter Thirty-Three	The Agents Return	344
Chapter Thirty-Four	Pact With The Devil	353
Chapter Thirty-Five	Westminster Bridge	363
Chapter Thirty-Six	Cabinet War Rooms	373
Chapter Thirty-Seven	MI5	385
Chapter Thirty-Eight	Active Duty	394
Chapter Thirty-Nine	No Place Like Home	403
Chapter Forty	An Evening With Jack Comer	417
Chapter Forty-One	The Memorial Service	433
Chapter Forty-Two	Baby George Arrives	445
Chapter Forty-Three	Battle Of The Bulge	449
Chapter Forty-Four	Christmas Day 1944	455
Chapter Forty-Five	The Diaries	472
Chapter Forty-Six	Hope And Despair	483
Chapter Forty-Seven	The Savoy Hotel	488
Chapter Forty-Eight	VE-Day May 8th, 1945	504
Chapter Forty-Nine	June 1980	512
Principal Characters		524
Principal historical figures dramatised to add context		527

Introduction

'The Final Year' is the concluding second part of 'None Stood Taller'.

For Lily Heywood and her colleagues, the veil of secrecy that surrounded their work for the Special Operations Executive was so pervasive that it continued long after the war. They met in secret each year on the anniversary of the D-Day landings, the invasion that was such a vital part of their work. Their self-imposed secrecy was maintained for 35 years, until the 1980 reunion when Lily made the decision to confide in her godson, Charlie. He was aware that both his parents and his godmother had played a part during the war, but he had no knowledge of what their involvement had been.

Lily invited him to step back in time with her and experience first-hand those terrible years of the Second World War. Together they re-lived the period building up to D-Day, which culminated on that most momentous of days, June 6th 1944. Emotionally drained, they both welcomed the end of the day, but a part of Charlie now remained in 1944. He had no option, two weeks later he was compelled to return to Middlebourne. Another year of the war remains untold. He has to step back through the portal into 1944, and re-live with Lily that final year of the worst conflagration the world has ever seen.

The Story So Far

From the ashes of the Blitz, Lily Heywood embarked upon a serendipitous journey that ultimately found her standing alongside Edward, the Earl of Middlebourne. The Prime Minister, Winston Churchill, had personally charged Edward with the task of creating an SOE intelligence unit in the grounds of Middlebourne Manor. The purpose of that top secret unit was to research potential D-Day landing beaches. During that time of heightened emotions Lily's life is cast adrift, its direction dictated by the war. What she feels for Edward is a love that must not mention its name. In its place she finds herself in the arms of another. Against this backdrop, Lily, and all the personnel of SOE Station M, enter into what was the most significant event of their lives. D-Day marked the culmination of three years' intensive research, ever-increasing tension, and ultimately crushing responsibility.

In the midst of that momentous day, there came the terrible news that the Gestapo had captured Agent Sparrow. For Lily and her assistant Fiona, the loss of their dear friend Dorothy was the most tragic event imaginable. Both women were completely devastated, but they remained determined to see the day to its conclusion. When darkness finally fell upon the longest day, Lily had given everything she had. With a heavy heart, she surrendered to the world of restless sleep and tormented dreams.

Chapter One
The Morning After

Charlie sat down opposite me. I could see he was unable to conceal his sense of anticipation as he spoke. "It must have been such a relief for you all when D-Day was a success. I suppose the final year of the war must have been a bit of an anti-climax."

"It was the exact opposite, Charlie. That final year was the longest year of my life, so many things happened."

"Do I assume then that Station M was given another assignment?" asked Charlie.

"It was, we had a lot to do with the V1 and the V2, in fact Edward was very nearly killed by one. I even worked for a short time as a field agent."

"You were an agent?"

"Don't sound so surprised, Charlie. Nothing I did compared with your mother's exploits; it was just something else that had to be done. When I look back, that final year was the most momentous of the war. I can't begin to describe the joy we all felt on the 8th of May 1945 when it was finally over. But that's not how the final year began, the morning after D-Day was one of the most sorrowful I have ever experienced."

I continued to describe the events of the following morning. I was half awake when there was a knock on my bedroom door. My bed clothes were tangled beneath me, damp with sweat and clinging to my body. Florence came in quietly with my cup of tea as usual, placing it on my bedside table. She always took great pride in her appearance, and that morning was no exception. Her golden hair was drawn back into an elegant bun, covered only by her maid's headband. Her crisp white pinny crackled with starch. She would ordinarily throw the curtains wide and greet me with a cheery smile. That morning she glanced aside, trying to conceal her expression.

"What's wrong, Florence?"

"I'm sorry, I'm upset."

"I can see you're upset and you've been crying. You're not fretting about the baby, are you? I told you I'll help you."

"It's not that, Mrs Heywood, I've just taken Miss Robinson a cup of tea. She was in tears, she told me about Dotty. I'm sorry, it's awful what's happened. Dotty was wonderful, she was always so nice to me."

I couldn't bring myself to answer her, I could only gesture an acknowledgement with a sorrowful expression. Florence looked so downhearted, and neither of us had adequate words for the situation. We had all lived through one of the most momentous days in British history, and yet there we were, both unable to mention it. She noticed my dishevelled bed clothes.

"You've had a restless night, I'm not surprised. I'll change the bedding for you."

Florence laid out my clothes for the day, and when I returned from the bathroom, she sat me down at my dressing table and started to do my hair for me.

"I can't believe it, Mrs Heywood, Dotty was so much larger than life, it doesn't seem possible she's gone."

"I feel the same, I can't stop thinking about her. I can't believe she won't walk into my office this morning."

"Do you know what happened?"

"We think so, she was so brave, she … "

Seeing I couldn't continue, she placed her hands on my shoulders for a moment before continuing with my hair.

"It really pains me to see you like this. If there's anything I can do, Mrs Heywood, anything at all, please ask."

"You're such a support to me, Florence, I can't imagine how I'm going to manage without you, when the baby comes."

Her expression changed, her sad eyes widened, and she looked away from me. I was left to speculate whether she had thought through just how much her life was about to change. I thanked her with a hug, and she left looking very dispirited. It was only moments later when Fiona knocked on the door. We said good morning to each other as if it was a day like any other, but this was not like any other day. Her eyes were red and her face pale and drawn, she had made no attempt to disguise her appearance with makeup.

"Can you face some breakfast, Fi?"

"Yes, I suppose so."

We walked in silence towards the Dining Room. Eventually Fi looked at me, her face portraying every emotion I was feeling.

"She's gone, Lily, we've lost her."

"I know," was all I could say.

Finally, we mentioned the invasion, but we were like two people at a wake making polite conversation about how nice the sandwiches were. Upon entering the Dining Room, we inevitably encountered Mr Jennings. Despite the momentous events taking place in Normandy, he remained resolutely calm and professional.

"Good morning, Mrs Heywood, Miss Robinson. What would you like for breakfast?"

Mr Jennings was a role model of self-control and discipline, he left us with no option but to snap out of our malaise. There were many occasions when he inspired me to overcome my personal doubts and fears, but none more so than that morning. He poured our tea, and while doing so he revealed that His Lordship had told him about Dorothy.

"May I be permitted to express my sincere condolences. I appreciate how close you both were to Miss Archer. She is a tragic loss."

"Thank you, Mr Jennings. I hope we can cope today, we're both struggling to come to terms with it."

"I have not the slightest doubt you will both cope admirably, Mrs Heywood. Dorothy did not fail in her duty and I cannot imagine for a moment that you are about to dishonour her valour by failing in yours."

His words reverberated right through me, I had to put my cup down before I dropped it.

"You're an inspiration, Mr Jennings, thank you."

"If that will be all, I shall instruct Cook to prepare your scrambled eggs."

As Jennings was leaving, Edward was just coming into the Dining Room. I presumed he had been over to Hut 3 to assess the latest information. He must have had little sleep, but he looked as impressive as ever in his immaculately tailored three-piece suit. He briefly discussed breakfast with Jennings before coming over to us. Edward then amazed me, he came directly to where I was sitting, and put his arms out, inviting me to stand up, upon which he put his arms around me and held me close! For several seconds his embrace felt as if he was comforting me, but then it was much more, his face was touching mine and his hands caressed my body. He then reacted as he suddenly realised what he was doing.

"That was terrible news about Dorothy, I am so sorry, how are you coping, Lily?" he asked.

I was so surprised, it did more than anything to jolt me out of my despair. Such an outgoing gesture of affection was most unusual, I was unsure how to respond. He then gave Fiona a comforting hug. She was pleasantly surprised and thanked him for his understanding. He was genuinely concerned and caring, I was deeply touched. Edward had only momentarily sat down when Lady Caroline entered the Dining Room. He immediately sprang back to his feet. Even dressed casually for breakfast, Caroline retained her wonderful ability to float into the room with consummate poise and elegance.

"Good morning, Mother, how are you this morning?" he said, as he held the dining chair for her.

"Good morning, Edward, Lily, Miss Robinson. Yes, I'm fine, thank you, I suspect I slept better than you last night."

"Yes indeed, it was a momentous day," replied Edward.

"What a pleasure to have you join us for breakfast, Miss Robinson."

"Good morning, Lady Caroline," Fiona replied.

"I am desperate to hear the latest news from Normandy, but first may I say how sorry I am to hear about your friend Dorothy. I believe you were all extremely close."

"Yes we were," Fiona replied, "Dotty was a remarkably special person, she shone a light in our lives..." She stopped abruptly. I could see Edward was conscious of our discomfort.

"I have just come back from Hut 3," he said, "there's a lot of information coming in. We need to assess the situation this morning just as soon as you are both ready, but it begins to look as if we have established our beachhead. If we can maintain and reinforce that position today - well, you know what that means, ladies, it will mean we have succeeded!"

I knew what Edward was doing, he was trying his best to deflect our attention and lift our spirits. That day of all days, we had to focus our thoughts. Mr Jennings' wise words were still ringing in my ears. He was right, D-Day had been the single most important day of our lives. Not even Dotty could obscure that. If Edward was correct, then everything we had been working towards had been a success. Slowly but surely the enormity of what we had achieved dawned upon us.

We hurriedly finished our breakfast and made our preparations for the day. As soon as we were ready, the three of us walked over to Hut 3 together. The weather was still unseasonal with a cold breeze, the long grass in the distance undulating like waves on the sea. We hunched our shoulders against the chill and hurried our footsteps. As we approached the hut, I could see from a distance that it was the usual hive of activity inside. They were all busy analysing the avalanche of information that was now pouring in.

The moment we stepped inside it was obvious that they had enjoyed little sleep. Rolo looked as if he hadn't been to bed at all, his thick glasses magnifying his bloodshot eyes. None of the men had shaved nor even changed their clothes from the day before. Woody retained his bow tie, albeit twisted to one side. Maggie at least had made an effort, but her makeup did little to disguise her drawn face. Despite their aching fatigue, the buzz of activity and tension was as high as ever.

"Morning, ladies, Edward," said Woody.

"Morning, everyone," I replied, "what's the news?"

"So far so good," said Patrick.

"We failed to capture Caen, and it looks like the Germans are counterattacking there," said a worried-looking Woody.

He looked a little like a casualty of war himself, so I walked over and gently straightened his bow tie.

"How serious is that?" Fiona asked.

"It's a setback, we need the Caen-Bayeux road to advance out of the beachhead," replied Woody.

"What are we doing about it?" inquired Edward.

"Montgomery arrived in the early hours this morning, he's ordered the 3rd British division and the 3rd Canadian division to press home the attack," replied Woody.

"What are we up against?"

"It's a part of the 12th Panzer Division, do you remember Colonel Kurt Meyer that I told you about? Nasty piece of work."

The conversation bounced back and forth as everyone offered whatever information they had. Their level of stress did not differ from the day before. Rolo was still rushing in and out of the communications hut, everyone was scrambling for maps or paperwork. There was the same D-Day atmosphere of heightened tension in the room; it was etched deeply upon their faces. The unrelenting stress combined with the lack of sleep had taken its toll on us all.

"Can I make a suggestion?" I asked.

Corky was shouting across the room towards Woody. Patrick was waving his arms in the air trying to attract Rolo's attention, nobody heard me. I picked up a large reference book and dropped it down onto a tabletop with a loud bang. Everyone stopped what they were doing with a startled expression. They stood in silence, looking at me.

"Can I make a suggestion? D-Day was yesterday," I said. "We've accomplished our mission. There's nothing we can do now that will change the course of the war, it's up to the generals and the troops on the ground. Don't you think you've earned the right to slow down a little?"

"You sound just like me Mammy, Lily," responded Patrick, "and she was *always* right."

They looked at each other like a bunch of naughty school-boys caught scrumping.

"You're right, Lily," said Corky, "we've done it, haven't we, so we don't have to run about like headless chickens any more."

"Have any of you had any breakfast?" I asked.

"Why don't we all go over to the canteen and have a cup of tea," Fiona suggested.

They were reluctant to tear themselves away from the incoming stream of information, but eventually everyone agreed. One by one we stepped out of the hut, and the chill breeze was a stark reminder that there was a world beyond Hut 3. Very little was said as we set off together towards the canteen. The trees in the distance swayed in the breeze, seemingly beckoning the clouds as they skated across the sky. We may have been heading in the direction of the canteen, but they noticed nothing, their minds were still back in Hut 3, analysing data. We were a sorry-looking bunch as we entered, each of us deep in our own thoughts. Brenda came over with a cheery smile and a tray full of cups, quickly followed by her enormous enamel tea pot.

"Tea for everyone?" she asked. "And what about a bacon sandwich?"

"You know the way to a man's heart, Brenda," replied Edward.

Brenda's smile was always irresistible, but never more so than that morning. She was a large woman with a permanently happy disposition. Her notorious smile had a way of convincing you that her bacon sandwich was utterly irresistible. People might think we should have had a glorious celebration the day after D-Day, well we did, that was it - in the canteen! The incongruous sight of Edward eating a bacon sandwich in the canteen, dressed in his immaculate suit, almost sufficed to raise a smile on my face. One by one, I watched their shoulders loosen, as the glimmer of a smile returned to their faces. Brenda was right, I don't think a bacon sandwich had ever tasted better.

We discussed every aspect of the invasion, and although an enormous amount of information was still coming in, it appeared to be a success from our perspective. Omaha Beach was our only doubt, could we have done more, did we miss anything? Woody especially felt a significant burden of responsibility. It was too early to make such judgments, but Omaha was nearly a disaster, something had gone badly wrong. Corky added a sobering comment.

"Did anyone seriously think the largest amphibious landing in history was going to stroll up the beach unopposed? There were always going to be heavy casualties."

He was right, but that inevitability was something we tried not to dwell on during those years of planning. Now the consequences were becoming clear, and the human cost became a stark and painful reality.

"Our job was to ensure the most effective landing, and therefore the least casualties," Edward said. "We have succeeded, we are ashore in Normandy. Perhaps the casualties we have suffered were the least that was possible."

"What about our people, Mac?" Woody asked. "Have you accounted for them all yet?"

"Not directly, no. We know every mission was a success, at least to some degree. I'm sorry, Lily, Sparrow is our only known casualty, but Goldfinch is also missing with no word. I'm very concerned about him, it's possible he was captured as well."

"Why are the others not reporting in, Mac?" Maggie asked.

"All of our people were on operations within ten miles of the landing beaches, they're slap in the middle of a battle zone now."

We sat there for well over an hour before returning to the hut. We were all aware of Dotty, she was in everyone's thoughts. But slowly that great British antidote to any tense situation emerged, as one funny comment followed another. There was an elephant standing in the corner of the room, but somehow we all negotiated a path around it. My lovely boffins were doing their best to lighten the situation.

"We still have work to do, but Lily's quite correct, we *can* slow down a little," said Edward.

"What about reconnaissance?" asked Maggie.

"Yes, we will need to assess the outcome of every recommendation we made. Hopefully, the world will never see an invasion on this scale again, but we must make sure we learn from our success as well as our failures. I suggest we start our reconnaissance flights tomorrow. Will you coordinate that with Wing Commander Albright, Maggie?"

"Yes, of course."

"I *will* get our people back," said Mac.

He realised what he had said, and he looked at me and Fiona.

"It's all right, Mac," I replied, trying to appear in control.

It was such a strange time for us, the sense of anti-climax

had become enormous. None of us seemed able to let go of our commitment towards D-Day. Somehow we had to embrace the new reality, which was the battle for Normandy and greater Europe. I suddenly realised that Fiona and I had become a distraction and our presence in Hut 3 wasn't helping that process. Everyone was aware how close we three were, each sharing our pain. I remembered what Jennings said about Dotty and I was not about to dishonour her valour by neglecting my own duty.

"Come on, Fi, let's leave them to it, shall we?"

Edward was staying there in the hut and he surprised me again by reaching out and momentarily taking hold of my hand.

"I'll see you later, Lily," he said, as he gently ran his fingers over mine.

We left with no fanfare, there weren't the usual screwed up balls of paper thrown at us, nor even one of Patrick's eloquent parting farewells.

"Edward's being really demonstrative, isn't he," Fiona said.

"He is, I don't know what's come over him."

There was one vantage point along the way back to the Manor from where you could see the estate office. When we reached it, I glanced in that direction, as did Fiona. We both saw Greg's Bedford van parked outside.

"Go to him, Lily, no-one will notice."

"I'm not sure if I can, Fi."

"I'm not sure that you *can't*, you need him right now."

I wasn't sure what I wanted. All I knew was that Edward was always there filling my every thought, but despite all my doubts and reservations I found myself turning towards the estate office. All my working life I had fought against my demons. I tried so hard to be in control, and yet there I was, cast hopelessly adrift on the sea of life, at the mercy of the waves. I wanted to be with Edward, but I was drifting towards Greg. Raising my arm to knock on his office door felt like an involuntary action that I was compelled to do. When he answered, I just melted into his arms.

"Damn, I've missed you," he said. "Tell me everything you can."

We hugged and kissed as if we had been apart for a year. He was like a soothing balm, the more we embraced, the more my body relaxed. Our embrace grew ever more passionate, but I couldn't go on.

"No, I'm sorry, I can't, just hold me."

"Have I done something wrong?"

"No, Greg, it's not you, it's Dotty."

"What's Dotty got to do with it?"

I broke away from him and sat down, my head in my hands.

"She's dead, Greg."

"Oh no! No, she can't be!"

He didn't ask me how or when, we had become that close, he instinctively knew how I felt.

"Would you like a cup of tea?"

"No, I won't, thank you. I seem to have been drinking tea all morning."

"To hell with tea," he said as he picked up a bottle of whisky.

"I can't drink whisky at this time of the day," I said.

"The only time when you can't drink a glass of whisky is at your own wake."

He poured two glasses of single malt whisky and added exactly the right amount of water to achieve the sweet spot that he knew I liked. I raised the glass to my lips, and despite the early hour, whisky had never tasted better. He didn't ask me about Dotty, he waited for when the moment was right for me. When I was upset, he kissed me; when I was feeling tense, he held me close. Greg could read my mind like an open book; he had a way of responding to my every need. I absorbed his affection like blotting paper and realised I had never confided in a man like that before.

"Shall I make you some lunch?" he asked.

For a moment I wanted to say yes, but suddenly realised I had forgotten Fiona.

"Oh Greg, I've left Fiona alone. You know how much I want to be with you, but I can't leave her alone, not now. Please forgive me, but I must go."

"Of course, I understand, will I see you tonight?"

"Yes!"

I reluctantly left the comfort of his arms and made my way back to the office. Perhaps it was the whisky, or maybe it was just Greg. Whatever it was, I no longer felt as if I was dragging my shadow behind me. As I approached the Grand Entrance, I saw Corporal Harris on guard duty by the door.

"Well done, Mrs Heywood, bloody well done!" he said with an enormous grin.

"I'm sure I don't understand what you mean, Corporal."

"I'm damn proud of you, all of you. What a day! This will be the end of that bastard Hitler, and you have all played a part."

"*Corporal Harris,* you're not supposed to *know* what goes on here!"

"I know nothing, Mrs Heywood. I thought that me standing here was just a military exercise."

"What am I going to do with you, Corporal?"

"Well, I could make a suggestion."

It was the first time since the news of Dotty that a genuine smile came to my face. It was only a fleeting moment, but I was grateful to Harris for it.

"This sounds like you might be about to make one of your inappropriate comments, Corporal."

"As if a chap like me would make an inappropriate comment to a fine lady such as yourself. Although I was wondering… "

"Don't say it, Corporal!" I replied, wagging my finger at him.

I had a wonderful rapport with Harris, he always made me

smile and I needed it more than ever that day. I knew he was a friend of Dotty's, but I couldn't bring myself to tell him. He'd raised my spirits and it was not the right time. I went on my way to the office and found Fiona sitting at her desk. I could see from her eyes she had been crying.

"Sorry, Fi, I didn't mean to be away so long. Let's have some lunch together."

"You look better for seeing Greg," she said. "You two work well together."

"We do, don't we?"

Neither of us was in the mood for a deep conversation, but she had made me think. Florence brought us some sandwiches and put the plates on my desk, though we hardly needed them after our bacon sandwich. Her expression hadn't changed from the morning, she appeared very sad and preoccupied. She was about to go, but I asked her to stay for a while.

"Is something wrong, Mrs Heywood?"

"No, Florence, would you sit down for a moment?"

"Am I going to be dismissed?"

"No, certainly not, but I need you to forgive me, Florence. I need to break our confidence."

"Our confidence?"

"Yes, I have to tell Miss Robinson."

"Tell me what?" Fiona asked.

"Florence is in the family way, Fi!"

"What! Oh Florence, you silly girl," Fiona replied without thinking.

Poor Florence was mortified. There was only one outcome for a pregnant housemaid in those days, especially an unmarried one. She would be dismissed immediately and left to fend for herself. We were all very aware of that.

"I want to help her in any way I can, Fi, so I'm going to need your help."

"Yes, of course. Well, the first thing you need to do, Florence, is to ask the father what he is going to do about it."

"I've already told her that. Have you heard from Harry?"

"No, I've written to him, but no reply yet."

"He's serving in North Africa, isn't he? He might not reply for ages," I said. "You need to approach his parents soon. I don't think you should leave it for weeks."

"I agree," said Fiona, "how many weeks are you?"

"It's three months, well, a bit more really!"

"Oh dear, are you starting to show yet?"

"I am a bit, but I can cover it up."

"Lily's right, Florence, you must approach either your parents or his."

"Florence can't go to her mother," I said, "it has to be Harry's parents. What are they like, Florence, are they a nice family, do you think they will take you in?"

"I don't like his father, he doesn't seem to approve of me, but I've got nowhere else I can go."

"You must see them as soon as possible," I said. "I'll go with you if you like."

"That's so kind, Mrs Heywood, but I should do it, shouldn't I?"

"Promise me you will do it soon."

"I will."

"I've told Florence I won't mention this yet, Fi. I'm afraid we need to keep this from Mr Jennings."

"I agree, we all know what will happen when he finds out!"

"I'm really grateful, Mrs Heywood, Miss Robinson, you're both being so kind to me."

She left the office looking slightly less downcast, but I still felt sorry for her. Her life choices had suddenly become drastically reduced, and she was only seventeen. After lunch we did our best to keep busy, trying to just act normally. Edward came in from time to time to give us the latest news from Normandy. All the while he was talking, my heart was pounding. I felt so guilty every time I was near him. The rough sea on which I was adrift seemed able to dash me against the rocks at any time of its choosing. I desperately hoped that he didn't notice. He was being so considerate to us both and that just made it all worse.

"Will I see you at dinner tonight, Lily?" he asked.

If I thought my heart couldn't beat faster, I was wrong. How could I possibly dine with Edward, and then go directly to Greg!

"Er, no, I'm sorry, Edward - I have to see my Gran tonight - that's right, isn't it, Fi?"

"Yes, that's right, Gran's expecting us."

Edward looked quite upset, he really wanted to have dinner with me. We should have celebrated D-Day together, but I just couldn't. Fi could read my mind, just as Greg did, she handled the situation well. As Edward left us, he tried to disguise his disappointment, but he wasn't entirely successful. This only served to make me feel worse. Fiona and I both had plenty of work to get done during the afternoon, but I had great difficulty concentrating. Every time I glanced over towards Fi, it would take her a moment to resurrect a faint smile. We weren't really achieving very much, even the telephones had fallen silent. It appeared that everyone's attention was directed towards Normandy. We decided to tidy up our desks and prepare to leave.

"I'd like you to come to Gran's, Lily."

"Yes I will, she'll have so many questions."

"We're both trying not to think about it, but there's something we have to do this evening."

I realised what Fiona was telling me. We had to tell Gran about Dotty.

"Oh my goodness, you're right."

We were both in denial about Dotty, pretending all was well. The realisation that we needed to tell Gran was when reality came calling. It started all over again, the terrible emptiness, the awful feeling that only grief can impose upon you. We stood there crying into each other's arms. We didn't want anyone to see us looking like that, so I suggested we quietly slip out and be on our way. Having narrowly avoided Joyce Evens and Jennings in the Great Hall, it was only William who caught sight of us. We said goodnight to him and stepped outside the Grand Entrance, walking quickly past the guard. We both must have looked dreadful, our mascara all over our faces. It was rather embarrassing when Rolo appeared running towards us. He ran so fast he was out of breath.

"What is it, Rolo, what's happened?"

"I've overheard a message between the Americans," he gasped. "They've picked up two Brits, they're trying to confirm their story."

"What story, what are you saying, Rolo?"

"The two Brits, Lily, they're saying they are SOE, *it's a man and a woman*."

"Oh good grief, it can't be!"

Fiona didn't say a word, she looked at me with her mouth open, her eyes like saucers. The next moment, she was running towards the communications hut. I looked at Rolo and we immediately ran after her. We arrived breathlessly at the hut to find Mac sitting with headphones on, and Susan scanning the frequencies. Fi grabbed him by the shoulder, shouting hysterically.

"Is it Dotty, is it Dotty?"

"I don't know," he replied, "but it sounds like it could be."

"Can we talk to anyone?" I asked.

"That's what I'm trying to do," he replied.

Having heard the commotion, Edward came rushing in. I struggled to catch my breath, let alone speak to him. Rolo told him what he had overheard, and Edward did what he always did, he calmly took control.

"Why are the Americans even interested in these people, Rolo?"

"I heard the Yanks say they looked suspicious. They were heavily armed and in civilian clothes and were seen abandoning a German military vehicle. It's suspected they may be fifth column."

"Who would the Americans contact about this, Rolo?" asked Edward.

"I'm not sure it would be a priority during the invasion, but I guess whoever has these people would probably contact the British field command."

"Right, send a message to Montgomery's staff, tell them it's possible that two of our agents are in the Americans' hands. Give them their code names. If they can confirm the names, then they are ours."

"I'll do it immediately," Rolo said.

He sorted through his files while we all just stood around. I was in a state of shock, hardly knowing what to think or what to do.

"Is it possible, Mac? Please tell me it's possible," I gasped.

"I don't understand how, but yes, I suppose it's possible. We don't know what happened to Goldfinch, except he was with Sparrow up to the point where she was apprehended. There's been no word from him. Starling clearly saw Dotty taken away by the Gestapo, so we mustn't get our hopes up."

"But it's a man and a woman; it *could* be Dotty and Rob, couldn't it?" Fiona said.

"It might also be any number of other SOE agents from the French Section who were operating behind enemy lines; there are other women involved."

"Oh my goodness, that's right, all the agents would have been overrun by advancing Allied troops," I said.

"That's right, so don't get your hopes up," replied Edward. "The only way it might be Dorothy is if she, and possibly Goldfinch, somehow escaped from the Gestapo."

We stood in silence again until I remembered what Dotty told me.

"I begged Dotty to be careful," I said, "and she said I needn't worry. She said she would find her way back to Middlebourne, even if she had to drag herself back by her fingertips. You know Dotty, *it's her, I know it is*, she'll find her way back."

Edward put his arm around my waist and looked into my eyes.

"I desperately hope it is her, Lily, but please don't make too many assumptions, it's too soon for that," he said.

That was the start of the most desperate period of waiting that I have ever experienced. Rolo sent his message to Montgomery's field headquarters, asking that the code names be given to as many field commanders as possible. It was a long shot. Everyone in Normandy had far more important things to do than to worry about our agents. Fiona and I just sat silently in Hut 3, everyone sitting with us in support. The hours ticked by painfully slowly. Every time a radio message came in, or the telephone rang, my heart stopped, only to beat faster in response to the disappointment.

"Look, Lily, Greg's coming over," Fiona whispered.

Greg came over to the intelligence section occasionally; he wasn't supposed to but he had signed the Official Secrets Act, and I turned a blind eye to it. My heart jumped when I saw him coming. If he came into the hut, it would be incredibly awkward, so I got up immediately and went out to see him. I had completely forgotten that he was expecting me that evening, but when I told him what was happening he understood. I didn't need to say anything; he realised that I didn't want him to embrace me, much less to kiss me in front of the boys in the hut. We spoke briefly, and I went back to join the others, feeling I was concealing something dreadful. My guilt was all-consuming, I even tried to avoid eye contact with Edward.

"Has Norton got a problem, Lily?" asked Edward.

"No, no, it's nothing really."

"Is it that problem he had with the dairy, I've been dealing with that," said the ever-loyal Fiona.

"Yes, it was."

"He's a good man, Norton, you were right, Lily. He puts in some long hours, doesn't he," replied Edward.

Standing there, having just told Edward a barefaced lie, I felt cheap and contemptible. I didn't even have the courage to look up at him, despising myself for what I had become. This was how that evening progressed, with Edward being wonderfully considerate, and me doing my very best to avoid him. Eventually, and with great reluctance, he excused himself, saying that dinner was arranged with Lady Caroline. Edward was far too honourable to disappoint his mother. He almost pleaded with me to accompany him, but I made my excuses. Once again, he was very understanding, saying if I didn't join him later, he would come and find me. I wasn't just cast adrift on a rough sea, I was dashed against the rocks and sinking beneath the waves. When Edward left, I breathed a sigh of relief, Maggie must have seen me slump back into my chair.

"I can see what you're doing, Lily, you can't carry on like this," she whispered.

"Please don't tell me it's that obvious, Maggie," I replied.

"I'm afraid it is, at least it is to me!"

I shuddered at the prospect that my personal torment might be common knowledge to everyone. Dotty was currently at the forefront of everyone's mind, so for that moment at least, I contented myself that no-one else would pick up the subtle indicators that Maggie could see. She was expert at interpreting meaning from the slightest clue. Having put that difficult experience behind me, I settled in to wait for the message I was convinced would come.

The sun didn't set until 10.15 that evening; I sat watching the last glow of daylight clinging desperately to the leading edge of the approaching night sky. Soon it was only a memory dragged below the western horizon. In the isolation of darkness, the incoming messages seemed to grow in significance, becoming our only sensory connection to the world beyond Hut 3. The airwaves were full of radio traffic as events in Normandy continued apace. At first, every incoming message made my heart jump. Then gradually, as the evening turned into night, the realisation that we might be in for a long wait became our reality.

Woody was asleep, slumped over his desk, while Patrick kept dropping his head and waking with a start. Fiona was desperate to stay, but she knew that Gran would be beside herself worrying where she was, she had to go. Reluctantly, Woody excused himself, as did Corky. Finally, Patrick persuaded me to give in and go to bed. Rolo, bless him, said he would share the night shift with Susan, the radio operator. Thanking them for their support, I made my weary way out of the hut. The blackout blinds were very effective, the moment the hut door closed the only available light was gone. Feeling my way along in the dark without a torch, I had no idea where I was going! Would I turn right towards Greg, or would I turn left towards the Manor. Knowing Edward would look for me, and with no conscious thought, I turned left.

Chapter Two
The Exquisite Moment

Before D-Day, none of the household staff would have dreamed of mentioning anything to do with the intelligence section. Now that the invasion was a reality, it was as if our self-imposed shroud of secrecy no longer existed. I found it very disquieting, secrecy was such an integral part of our work, it permeated everything we did. The newspapers and wireless covered every detail of the invasion, but it seemed that the household staff apparently knew what our role had been.

With hindsight, it was silly to think the staff had no idea about our work. Of course they understood we were a secret military establishment, but I deluded myself into thinking they would not question our involvement. It shocked me to be congratulated by so many of them. I was almost expecting it from cheeky Corporal Harris, but I didn't expect Mary to congratulate me.

"Good morning, Mrs Heywood, isn't it wonderful news?" she said. "You must all be so relieved, and proud of what you have achieved."

"You're not supposed to be aware of these things, Mary!"

"I'm sorry, Mrs Heywood, we know nothing really. I just know you've got a lot to do with D-Day, and I'm so proud of you!"

"Bless you, Mary. You do realise that you must never say a word about this? None of the staff can say anything."

"That's something you need never worry about, Mrs Heywood, there's not a single person here who would ever let you down."

I thanked her for her kind words, everyone was being so supportive and understanding towards Fiona and me. It was such a comfort during that anxious time. There had been no news about the two Brits in American custody, but we both clung resolutely to our conviction that they would prove to be Dotty and Rob. Each time the other agents managed to send us messages, our conviction grew stronger.

As the battle for Normandy raged on, our reconnaissance and analysis were stepped up. Johnny Albright brought us back wonderful photographs of the landings, and Maggie analysed them as usual. The boys wanted to know every detail of the invasion, and the subsequent re-supply. Superficially, it was business as usual, but it was a dreadful few days for Fiona and me. The tension was unbearable, my heart continued to race every time the telephone rang or there was a knock on my door. Our torment was finally laid to rest on the afternoon of June the 12th.

It was one of those exquisite moments in life when an unassailable memory is forged with such clarity that it transcends the decades. Fiona and I could hear a commotion coming closer to the office. We looked at each other with alarm. With the ruckus growing louder and louder, Fiona and I looked at each other with concerned expressions. Edward burst through the door, rapidly followed by the boys from Hut 3, together with Mac, four of our field agents, and Susan the radio operator.

"It's Dotty and Rob!" shouted Rolo.

What followed can only be described as a spontaneous outpouring of emotion. It was an unspoken truth that none of us allowed ourselves to celebrate the success of D-Day. We